THE TERRIBLE FRIGHT

JACK KELLY

DEDICATION

For
The River &
The City

ACKNOWLEDGMENTS

Thanks for the Internet, Google Search
and Wikipedia for assists large and small.

Thanks also to ADW
who read all three stories
providing helpful comments,
suggestions and clarifications
as needed.

AUTHOR'S NOTES

New Orleans is the setting and a character in this story.
No effort to accuracy was attempted in measuring
distance, direction, or time.
All faults are intentional and strictly the author's
who thinks he's being clever.

Been Named

Been named now

     Given title as a more accurate telling of the tale perhaps and beside the point entirely and whether it is name or title now is irrelevant with its current frequent use and reuse.

     A name given without asking and now so common or has become common enough through near constant misthought and misuse as to have become an actual name and morphed from an original and mistaken identity to now actually being her name. Still unasked for, still uncalled for as she'd always preferred, as opposed to this hasty baptism, this unofficial anointing of the scary inexplicable thing in the dark in the attempt to explain the scary thing away. A label for the portion of the dark which is grinning back at you, which you cannot otherwise describe and forever more hope to never encounter. Much preferring to skip the firsthand experience in an inherent understanding how some encounters are better left forever unmade and with whatever luck you can muster or spare on it.

She still preferred things as they'd been before all this nuisance and noise about it. What's in a name after all other than its use to pin things down or to provide a hazy resolution and so much pop psych bullshit with its still lone, if fatal, flaw as no one ever asks what to do if you cannot find it. Besides, go reference Ol' Bill and see what he wrote up about this naming business after all and see how it turned out for his cast of characters. All kinds of things fit her so much better and she did like it so much more. The anonymity suiting her better like a superior cut of cloth if you will. This statement she found she much rather favored but like the not so famed Greek Titan Epimetheus as a possible patron and strong counter point to his more famous brother Prometheus.

Still, the cry rises from her victims, from the few survivors or more likely scattered and distant witnesses. Reference points for those who weren't there and who still seek to put a past tense blanket of understanding over events which do not readily offer any up. It seems it has come to pass how she should reside as more than a passing shadow in the night, the darkness inside the darkness. It is perhaps another cliché to boot. But it doesn't otherwise alter what seemingly has been decried. How she should rise a legendary haunt in a city which boasts more than enough already to have earned its self-conferred title of 'most haunted' and was mostly without the need of another.

Sorry, a little segue there. She's been experiencing a little trouble staying focused. She keeps getting lost in damn stray tangents as she sits in her worn and torn blacks upon a rare pristine perch of a doorway deep in the Quarter, waiting for the sunlight to tell her it's long past time to go. It's time now for all haunts large and small, like her, to return back to whatever patch of ground which will have them lest they be caught out in the daylight and in the easily frightened gaze of a largely skittish humanity.

Any name will do. She tosses the phrase back around in her mind though she'd rather not. It's not for her you understand. It's a damn unnecessary weight to boot which she can plain do without as she still could not give a good god damn less about it all.

If one is to become a haunt, a legendary whatever in a city readily accepting of such things. And apparently, it is a decision no longer hers if it ever was, then a near mythical name is called for and if it calls forth a sacrilege in any language or faith then so be it and so much the better. She mostly finds herself indifferent through all of the fuss being made, the importance of being named by others. It's so much made over so small a thing of consequence, something being made out of almost nothing at all.

Alright, a confession for a moment, a guilty pleasure to even admit to but she did so like the name chosen for her. She does wonder though as to the why of the particular selection. She appreciated the juxtaposition, the irony in the word play versus its other connotations. It pleases her more than she cared to admit to, reveling in the little touch of blasphemy attached to a name now whispered like a curse. A name given to her like it was a scourge of a designation.

She focuses on the delight in the rhythmic click-clack of her heels ringing off the pavement of the Quarter. The tickety-tock of the clock which serves her no more and which no longer informs her world. This is much to her delight and is revealed in a mirthful little laugh from her lips as she embraces the night. Her mirthful laugh morphs into one of pure menace. Menace of a psychotic sort were it defined in human terms and a phrase which no longer informs her world either anymore.

Well then, no rest for the wicked as the saying goes as she returns to the hunt and her duties to the city. So bring an army, bring whatever and all things you can when you come for her and she will pray you back into the arms of whatever deity will have you.

Been named now, a given name and all so close to a right proper noun with such delicious irony. Such a tasty morsel too, such the delight and so much beauty to behold in this haunt called by name now.

Been named now and for the rest?
Well, been warned now haven't you?

Sevens

Seven's a lucky number or so it's said but then there's the old rhyming line naming seven for the devil. It's a line from the book for counting crows which she recalls from some deep depth of memory though the original source remains unknown or lost to her along the way. The source is inconsequential one way or the other as it still bodes as an unhappy omen for an anniversary and a direct counter point to the very notion of lucky.

More years gone now and another anniversary approaches on the calendar. Another moot point mostly as it's simply another notch in the belt of time. Time passing looks different from this side of the in-between and she has grown accustomed to its lack of impact upon her. Its complete lack of meaning upon her now leaving her unable to determine if the length is nothing at all or ancient history long passed. Enough time passed now, she surmises, to bury some things. Enough time to have swept broken things out from under the rug and then out the door and down to the street as if the street would have them.

It's summer and already past the period described locally as being 'just a little warm.' The warmth turned now into plain straight hot in the annual seasonal turn where the rain which falls at least once a day as it ever does in the city. The rain falls with the urgency and quickness which is normal in this subtropical environment. It passes as fast as it had arrived leaving behind nothing but the steam rising from the sidewalks to set upon the city and really remind one of the grip of the swamp and other waters constantly held back out on the edges of the city's defenses. The rain brings a momentary retreat indoors where ill deeds can be done in the comforts of one's home behind closed doors and away from the steam and the heat which rule the city this time of year.

Newspapers blow about and land at her feet stopped for a moment as she sits on a bench in black leather oblivious to or immune from the heat. She is an incongruity in comparison to the tourists and the sensible natives in shorts and thin t-shirts which pass her by pretending to not see her there. Her arms stretch out to claim the tip of the bench in either direction as her head tilts back on her neck. Her sunglass covered eyes stare straight up to the clear blue sky with nary a cloud to disrupt its endless expanse in the gap between showers on one side of the street and the sun still shining on the other.

She'd kill for a trickle of sweat, for enough heat to enable the natural phenomenon in her person while wondering if she'd tan or burn or if it would turn all of her leather encased fair flesh of hers a bright lobster red right before the blistering took hold. She sits still enough on the bench to be mistaken for one of the many living statues seeking money from the tourists which populate the Quarter. If she had a hat to lie at her feet she might collect some monies too. When she looks down after a moment so long she doesn't properly know how long it actually was, she sees a few dollars in her lap including a five and the monies there raise a smile on her face. Beer money she thinks and an excellent idea as she collects the monies there, slipping the coins and all into her pockets without the bother of counting. The amount collected is of no matter as long as she has a dollar so she can snag a tallboy from one of the many small convenience stores scattered throughout the Quarter. So life is good, if only for a moment.

The next morning there's a nightstick in her ribs coupled with a shout to get up and move along. She's being rousted with the rest of the drunks and homeless who populate Lafayette Square across from the federal courts because none can stay here. It wouldn't do for the tourists to see them, it wouldn't do at all. She stumbles along in the first daylight looking for the pathway which leads to her spot hidden away from the world to wait until dark to resume her crawl about after the heat has passed. Pickings are slim this time of year as it's too damn hot for the tourists and the natives all have sense to stay indoors behind their curtains and AC. If they've got the dollars, they get out of town to return in time for the start of the South's second passion, football season, 'who dat' indeed.

The constant thrum of the fans and air conditioning unmindfully accompany her as she shuffles along off the modern streets of what was at one time called the American sector of the city and across Canal and into the ancient flagstone streets of the Quarter. She likes the delineation even if it's an outdated idea which theoretically no longer applies to a city normally resistant to any application of the term *modern*.

It's an unofficial demarcation which she especially appreciates for its lack of markings and stances at grandeur, a physical representation of her current situation in the in-between in a more tangible form. She can always tell when she's crossed this line marked as it is with a four lane street plus the neutral ground and streetcar. The pour of modern concrete and asphalt between lines of taller buildings act as a clear benchmark where one is no longer on this side or in the area where the rules are slightly differently applied and understood than they are over here.

Or so she thinks as she crosses the boulevard and heads down towards Jackson Square with her head down. Her hands deep within the pockets of her stolen black leather jacket, pardon reclaimed jacket she's rescued from abandonment. It had been left to sit on a bench all by its lonesome when she came across it way back when.

Clear lines and what she wouldn't give for them. Some form of clarification or guideline. Some clear marking serving to delineate sides could act like some signpost even if it were like one out of a warped episode of the twilight zone. She thinks it might be right at the top of the list on paradoxical statements of pure oxymoronic, uncut.

She's long ago given up on explanation in any form for this variation of existence and instead embraced the concept where there is no why to it, let alone rhyme or reason. She is a little tired though of her testing the boundaries through the method of accidental discovery or, had back when she'd been new at this whole in-between thing and had bungled about in the night. Now she preferred the cover of night for so many reasons she could no longer recall why she'd have ever taken the path of the sun. All of the night is hers to call, to wander and revel in it like a second home.

She feels like she's caught up in some twisted narrative confused about its settings and her place amongst them. Still they stretch and cling to her unwilling to let her go or leave her in peace or to her own devices. Bothersome is what it is. How it should engage in such activities when it doesn't otherwise give a single damn about her now or before this intervening in-between. How it begrudges her this placement of hers interrupting the otherwise incessant natural flow of things in the wash of time.

She sighs and shudders from a cold without source which clings to her despite the heat of the summer as she closes in on her destination and her date with the golden comforting warmth of Mr. Jack. Mr. Jack provides no answers and asks no questions within his ambered waves. Mr. Jack offers relief from her confusion and a simple delicious warmth and a comforting sing-song of forget-me-pleases which in turn pleases her. The nice blur to soften and dulls memories which will never be lost or forgotten. The relentless picture perfect memory of hers, sharp as ever and this is her true punishment. There's no escaping it for even rare small moments despite Mr. Jack's offer of a pleasant blur. Never enough however, to completely obscure the otherwise disturbing images which float freely through her mind clear in every detail.

The world should stop its clinging she thinks, should stop its pestering insistency. There should be some kind of relief for her from its pressing need, its determination to calling to her when she's already so tired despite her agelessness.

She can hear The Man of the Waters calling to her and thinks to slip beneath the waves, thinking how peaceful it must ultimately be. She's thinking hard about sliding away despite not knowing if it's a possibility for her. Perhaps a fade out is more likely. A return to insubstantiality but she doesn't like the idea of it at all.

She doesn't like the idea of the long slide of decay. Better this way, she thinks to go out on top and become another mythical and never believed to have been a haunt, in this city famed and self-titled as most haunted.

Seven is the devil. A line from the old counting rhyme bouncing through her mind as she downs her tall shot of Jack. The ambered liquor warming her in its descent with the added benefit of taking the edge off most of her thoughts while sharpening others and one in particular. Her wandering distracted brain stretches out on its chain testing its boundaries before finding a comfortable place to roost at seven in the crow count. An appropriate spot in conjunction with the storm fast approaching.

Hurricane Isaac is the city's latest anniversary visitor moving ever closer to the city along the route which the killer Miss K took. From somewhere off in the background a familiar song plays which she's trying to ignore. The song is insistent like a pest and immune to being ignored like the storm which is closing in on the city. As storms are ever going to want to be doing as they have before, anniversaries be damned. It still feels like some form of bad omen or simply a try at black humor, gallows humor too as another storm comes to attempt the kill to finish the earlier coup attempt. Possibly proving the Mayans right and this is the end of the world and so much for happy anniversary.

Isaac comes like an exclamation point out of some twisted origin like he's late for a hot date bearing down upon her and her city in eerie likeness straight down to the day and possibly the hour of the previous grievous strike. The pressure of the storm's approach triggers unpleasant and jumbled mostly unclear memories to tumble turbulently about most unpleasantly in her mind. Flashes which make no narrative sense to her as she no longer has any ties to and serve to confuse her, which makes her feel personally persecuted like the storm is coming right for her to finish the job left undone by the bitch Miss K.

The one clear memory carved out from her confused and lost past is the memory of Miss K being the source of her current condition. The storm being her birth and a singularly hostile and disagreeable way to enter into the world and perhaps a hip pocket guide to psychology's explanation for her acting out behavior, which at least draws a laugh from her.

She doesn't need this storm or the reminders it dredges up in any shape, fashion or form. She could do without the unkind reminder worse than any scar. At least a scar fades over time occasionally allowing for it to be forgotten. This was something else entirely, the persistence of a never closing wound like some Greek gods punishment like ichor forever seeping and pain ever constant. Worse, it is right on the surface and in the open for all to see and pick at.

It didn't help how this was currently coupled with the feeling of something walking up right behind her trying to catch her unaware and is gone every single time when she turns round to catch it. Straight unnerving the idea of something, anything, which could cause the hairs to stand up on the back of the neck of a haunt itself. A thing she doesn't want care to even imagine as she can imagine horrible, ghastly beasties humongous in size and appetite.

A shudder up and down her spine like someone had walked across her grave, all the while knowing how it was a singular impossibility leaving her wondering if it still holds when the grave doesn't. It's a philosophical point best left to smarter people than she perhaps.

These are some somber thoughts, a lingering hangover like a fugue still clinging to her from her long sleep rudely disturbed but apparently not entirely shaken off. Calls for a shot of Jack she thinks as she moves deeper into the Quarter with a damn haunting musical like sound blowing on the wind in a sing-song of notes which come in and out without consistency but rather as a maddening float around. The notes pull at her for reasons which they keep to themselves without provision of any tell or clue to their origin or nature. Just the ever persistent tug at her as she looks around for their source to come away thwarted in her attempt.

An irritating distraction as she decides upon a course of ignoring the notes as they flit in and out of her range of hearing adding fuel to the rise in her anger, a pyre which needed no additional help in this endeavor. Something to worry about, she supposes, if it occurs again and never mind the hairs on the back of her neck are standing up. An unusual sensation for her in this new in-between existence. A haunt for a haunt, not so uncommon in this city she supposes and perhaps she shouldn't be surprised of other things out there in the dark of night which could even offer a scare or two along the way.

Nyctophilia

New Orleans is a city which actively embraces the night. The city has had a long history and preference for the dark despite occasional flirtations with the sunlight. They're simple dalliances, and all serve to make the night all the more delicious for having played at, for pretending to prefer the sunlight.

It's a mutual attraction often denied or played down and not at all advertised but clear in many examples throughout the city but most especially in her oldest portion, the original squared out area of the Quarter. One only has to look at the lamps in the Quarter as they struggle against the dark in deference to the city's preference. They strain their brightness as far as they can in open defiance to the city's natural love of the dark. Love of the dark, as loosely defined and perhaps stretched a bit into a new definition, a new reference point more akin with the so called Creatures of the Night and all of the other bumps which use the cover of dark for their activities.

Dark of night is such a wonderful phrase. It hides more than you think and yet, it's not as ominous a statement as it might sound were it typed or said aloud. Were it not for the menacing use of the same in all the horror classics as to have become an ingrained clichéd point. The dark hides all kinds of things for reasons both fearsome and banal and only seems fearsome in this form. Mind you, fearsome things have good cause and reason to seek the dark and stay there, to call it home. They finding comfort in the shadows away from the harsh sun's light of the long summer's day.

It's an apt phrase for a place lauded as The Most Haunted city in North America, as the city is occasionally billed and promoted, lending more credence for the city's love of the dark. The haunts of the city both great and small combined with the summer heat chasing everyone into the shadows and the cover of the night add to the congregation under the stars. It's a strange amalgamation of adherents under the moon ranging from tourists to the cities regular denizens along with the other mystic beings, and all without having touched upon the voodoo native to the city. All of the creatures of the night bumping up against those same and very real Creatures of the Night which normally stay down in the daylight to rise again at the call of the moon and such as she has now become. She is the darkness as an old turn of phrase but her perfect home now in the embrace of night, the sweet kiss of near permanent night. So beware the darkness sweetheart as there are all kinds of things bumping around within it.

The click clack of her heels mark time against the uneven pavement of the Quarter and echoes from off the walls of the buildings closet to her, beating a comforting tattoo for her, as she moves along her route. She's got a near full moon hanging in the sky tonight calling her to her duties, to her hunt but it feels more like a bad moon tonight and kin to the one CCR sang with the warning for all within the song's range to stay indoors or it could mean your life. She smiles her little wicked smile at the thought. At any thought at all of fearing for her life and a fear which had not been broached in some years now. It was a strange a notion to populate her thoughts tonight and suddenly the full moon feels ominous akin to the bad sign the great blues man Albert King sang about in his iconic oft covered song. She shrugs off the unnatural feel of omen as she buries her hands in her coat pockets. She's unconcerned for the moment as quite frankly the entire notion feels like it's been stolen from another character's story arc anyways and thus rightly to be left alone.

Her insatiable hunger has been too long denied and she's glad for the company as she undertakes her long neglected hunt once more to the far off strains of swamp music rising up with her. Some classic Zydeco or other local mix stirred into the regular cacophony of the Quarter. She feels blessed beneath the Goddess' impassive and unjudging light. Moon called and moon kissed. She soaks in the night air with her arms spread out at shoulder height with her palms upward in a greeting to the Goddess, to the Queen of Night. Asking her if she might grant her favor upon the activities her servant is set to perpetrate tonight.

The moon with her eternal double influence in this in-between life both as a creature of the night subjecting, however randomly, to the waxing and waning and her fickleness and the same waxing and waning effecting its pull over her as a woman. She is after all at some measure or definition or level still a woman, even if it could not be currently found or loosely defined. She hasn't lost it in this slide over to the other side.

She's both eager for and yet hesitant to start her hunt this evening because from somewhere deep within her she feels like these pleasures are numbered and in single digits and this one might be one of her very last. This gives her reason to pause, to take it slow, and to savor. To see if she cannot somehow stretch this out, make the joy last though the increased intensity through the savored action. She knows she's grasping here, there are no guarantees or certainties and still she reaches for it as unusual a thought as it might be as compared with the bulk of her time here in this in-between place. The reach, the try to brings a certain level of satisfaction to her simply for the striving and almost offsets the otherwise overwhelming melancholia. It's among the very last of these events for her and a further signal of her own undoing and impending demise.

Fuck, that's a morose and solidly unhelpful thought she thinks a little too out loud. Still it's more vexing distraction for her to deal with when her patience is strung out raggedly thin already. She'd never intended to cast such ill omen on the hunt or to put such a pall over it despite the bright moonlight which never quite reaches all the way down to the pavement or makes the Quarter any brighter. The whole love of the dark thing asserting itself once more.

She would take it all back if she could to remove the unintended insult to the goddess and the moon, in impassive permanence like any of it could ever matter to eternals such as they. Mostly she simply wishes to remove the damn near permanent chill which dances all along up and down her damn spine. More vexing to have a chill when ones' a haunt and alleged to be immune to such things.

She is, as ever, fortunate and blessed in strange fashions and increments by the goddess and the moon however it is the two of them decide these things. The randomness best exemplified by what happens next when she turns a corner. To be generous, call it a blind corner to obscure the fact she was simply not watching which way she was going or to who or what might be standing there in her path as she bounces off what feels like a damned wall or something equally solid and unmoving.

She looks up and is mildly surprised to see a muscle bound ape standing rudely in her path. How or when she'd reached this face off she didn't really know or care for that matter. She's still a little lost in her wanderings through the Quarter and not entirely certain where in the hell she exactly was in time and space let alone the in-between in this chance encounter.

Gorilla she thinks, as she examines him from the spot her ass selected on the pavement after running into him. It was an accident she thought, until she looked up at him standing in a practiced pose she was certain he'd determined before the mirror or at least in his mind as to be imposing. His presence is presenting her with an encounter she'd really rather not have right now, and would really rather avoid entirely.

She sighs. It seems he's determined to not allow her these options as demonstrated by his posturing to show her how strong he is and where his strength lies. She feels correct in her assessment of gorilla with all beg your pardons to actual gorillas. She recognizes this for what it is, a disguising of fear while this gorilla attempts to impress with his bulk defined and inflexible. This will soon to prove his undoing without him understanding he has already lost because his attempt has failed from the beginning. The gorilla doesn't understand this yet, doesn't understand because it has never occurred to him how all of this bulging muscle is only a disguise for strength and how strength can come in many other forms. He doesn't know how this is a very giant blind spot of his and how it has deceived him in a soon to be demonstrated fashion.

She reaches up a hand in the universal help a person up signal. The smug prick bastard ignores her as he folds his arms across his chest and smirks over at his buddy well pleased with his inside joke. This is to be as expected and she's not even disappointed in it. She takes her hand and places it back beside her hip to mimic her opposite hand at the opposite hip. She pushes herself to kneel and then to a squatting position muttering unkind things to herself. She's muttering to disguise how she's coiling herself up into a tensioned spring about to be unlatched while the much pleased with himself gorilla ignores her, much to his impending peril.

She's got her feet underneath her and can feel the power of her crouch in every muscle of her legs as they wait for the command to spring forth. She looks up past her sunglasses sitting askew on her face ruining her Corey Hart cool, ignoring the whole being on her ass on the pavement thing for a moment as counterargument to the notion.

The gorilla is laughing at her enjoying his little joke, enjoying it more with her seeming struggle to get her ass off the ground. He's saying something snide to his goon friend and, as the saying goes, well that tears it. She launches herself from her coiled spot straight at his eyes. Her nails are out like claws to swipe that shit eatin' grin right straight off of his damned face. Smug bastard, let's see how you pull the look off now, she thinks to herself. The bad pun intended and thank you very much.

The bastard screams in an unnatural register. Well, that's how she hears it or will tell it later at any rate while his goon buddy tries to pry her off of him but she's locked around the gorilla clawing and biting at his face. The gorilla's friend discovers this much to his horror when she turns to snarl at him with a mouthful of his gorilla friend's face in her mouth. Scraps of his friend's face dangle from her blood smeared teeth when she bears the feral snarl at the gorilla's friend. The friend backs away from her with a look of abject terror.

It's a departure for her from her usual coolness, her aloofness, forsaken now and left behind in the wake of her kiss and whatever power it possess and her typical mode of offense surprisingly unused. An atypical and unexpected decision by her to use her own preternatural strength instead as an ironic tool to utilize against this tool of a person. A bounty presented to her by the night. She's thankful for the pleasures of the hunt literally bumping into her like this. She'd been swerving towards dipping dangerously into a personal nadir, feeling sorry for herself and in certain need of this offering as a reminder to never indulge in the idea of it.

The gorilla stumbles then falls to his knees crashing down hard upon them with her riding him down while she works her way to his neck to the hole she'll tear there to deeply drink her fill of him. Drink she does, until there's a gurgle from the now spent gorilla she holds by his lapels or would, were he wearing anything other than a t-shirt. She looks over mildly surprised to find the gorilla's friend still standing there frozen at the horror witnessed though she doesn't blame him. She's sure she must look a fright after all as she smacks her lips.

Her face and upper torso are covered in fresh and deliciously warm blood and she's feeling a little dazed from the meal as she struggles to form a cognizant thought past the blood. She's deciding on the gorilla's friend's fate as she casually releases her grip and allows the remains of the first gorilla to fall away from her and against the building. She wipes her mouth with her the back of right hand and can feel her hair standing up all over the place like some warped fright wig or some such shit. She can feel her eyes large and ablaze with what would be described by anyone else who might see them, and previously had, as eyes which do not belong in the face of anything human.

She grabs the gorilla's friend by the back of his neck pulling him towards her. Her gore covered tongue snakes in and out to force apart his lips as she's on him. She wraps her entire person about him in a paralyzingly embrace too strong to break. Not that he wants to, not with her exquisite kiss pouring into every part of him and taking everything from him. Her kiss leaves him conflicted with the very real image of his buddy's blood which he can taste everywhere from her lips to between her teeth.

Her kiss moves deeper into his soul flooding every part of his being with her presence. It's an addition to his quickly dwindling confliction with the rise of his rock hard cock aching against his jeans and her leg with her probing, her insistence. It's a feeling of indescribable wonderment, an incredible orgasm as he shoots his load into his pants. She breaks the kiss long enough to laugh. It's a cackle which will ring through his ears and brain for the remainder of his, growing shorter by the minute, life as she takes everything from him.

She drops him down beside his gorilla buddy on the sidewalk just short of not quite dead. She reaches down to line him upright against the building next to the gorilla, two drunks passed out to anyone casually looking at the scene. He'll have a lot to explain to the cops when they find him lying beside the body of his gorilla buddy, covered in blood but without any ability to explain away any part of this crime. There's no defense short of insanity should he claim it to be the work of the haunt of a woman. A tale likely to not be believed and he's likely to later rot away in jail for the rest of his life.

It seems to take forever for the cops to arrive and he offers no excuse or defense when they roust him about to send him on his way until there is no response from his buddy beside him. The cuffs come out fast and are snapped on quickly as they take him away in their squad car. He's still looking over their shoulders and his to the echo of her boots on the streets somewhere where her wicked laugh is bouncing off of the walls of the buildings left and right.

She straightens herself up as best as she can short of a full on shower before stepping into the street making a quick turn up the next street and then down the other to give her some space away from the two gorillas before stopping to get her bearings. Surprisingly, she's deeper into the Quarter than she'd thought, though a little off the much beaten path which helps to explain the gorillas and their motivation in fronting her. They'd mistaken her for just another tourist lost and as an opportunity for them. She's deep enough into the Quarter to have actual private residences owned or rented around her. She examines the doorways and fences looking for one which is slightly less uninviting as she moves further down the street. Some steps further down she finds what she's looking for in a fence which is not as secure as it should be. She moves across the street to pry past the gate and into some poor bastards' courtyard, to wash the blood off in the fountain she finds there.

She's much pleased by the fortuitousness of her location and the fountain, staining the bricks of the patio around it with the stripped off blood and gore. She even dunks her head into the water and throwing her hair back in a purely decadent moment. She feels much blessed by the night as she twists the excess water from her hair looking up at the widows walk above her. The moon is shining on the roof tiles but remains otherwise unseen past the peak of the roof where a haunting mournful tune faintly carried finds its way across and down to her in the courtyard.

The tune has hints of a slightly metallic tone as it hangs in the air like a dirge, disturbing to no end and purely unnerving in the light of the mess of a murder done and not far from her present location. She feels suddenly self-conscious about the sloppy work of the kill made in a rush of pure anger. It was her most impressive power fueling her preternatural strength, and still a mess made in her distraction in a very public place. It was a mistake which is certain to come back and bite her solidly in the ass as a reminder how she really does need to pay more attention to these things.

She leaves the sanctuary of the courtyard still dripping leaving a trail of water behind her as she goes in search of the origin of the elusive taunting song to ask it what it could possibly want with her.

Fates Warning

She can more clearly hear the now distinct if short and slightly metallic mournful sound as it drifts about in a tormenting fashion out across the spaces of the Quarter. A sound like the one from the damn Charles Bronson movie where Henry Fonda breaks type and plays the bad guy. It's a sound you'd know if you'd ever heard it once. She turns to see what appears to be a clichéd form of an Ol' Blues Man standing there like an apparition or some other such spooky shit within a swirl of still clinging mists. It's as if he'd materialized or sprung up from the ground or somewhere else possibly. She did not wish to speculate upon, as all alternatives were dubious at best especially in light of her own situation as evidence enough.

She feels bedraggled, good word there, roughly hewn presently and not far removed from her most recent murder whose blood still speckled about her despite her stolen fountain wash. She's still rather sorry for the mess she'd made of it.

"Damn girl but aint you a sight now," he says looking about him for a spot to spit the wad of what she assumes is chewing tobacco out to the ground though it's nothing as nasty as that.

"You've gone and made a mess of things now aint you girl," he asks as he's looking at her like he's expecting a response from her but she's too caught in a moment of confusion to respond.

His tone is one of over familiarity with her and gives her pause while she tries to place the man and from where it was they'd encountered each other before. She surmises it was only in passing, though she cannot put her finger on the occasion.

She thinks to say something clever, to offer one of her trademarked smart-ass comments but is unable to conjure anything better than to ask him where his guitar is. The comment falls stupidly from her mouth before her better sense can stop such foolishness. Fortune smiles upon her as the man laughs a raspy age old laugh at her before telling her how he lost it when he washed down from Chicago some time ago. It's all right mind you, so long as he's got his harp to blow. He then raises said harmonica to his mouth, as an example she supposes, and begins anew with the damn creepy Sergio Leone piece setting a chill racing along her spine.

"So yeah girl," he continues on in his overly familiar way with her but she's distracted by this and keeps missing what he says because of it. She really needs to be concentrating on what she's being told. Hell, it might be important and she's already missed some part of it she knows.

And still, she wants to ask him if she knows him even though she knows it's perhaps the singularly stupidest question she could ask here as a contrivance to move the plot forward in full clichéd Hollywood fashion. She should mean how, how does he know her? It too seems such the cliché and would somehow be disappointing to the man. The notion she should be in any way worried about how this old man took to her further causes the rising of her ire at the situation. This coupled with her running annoyance at having been rendered momentarily speechless though she'll soon find a remedy for it.

"So old man," she asks in a clear tone specifically designed to communicate her displeasured state, "I guess were supposed to known one another then?"

She finishes the question less than satisfied with the out loud display as compared with how it had sounded in her own head. She's feeling somewhere between straight foolish and plain stupid with the asking of the question which falls with a thud to the pavement from the scorn of the old man's glance, a glance which proved her original point.

"You could say that girl," he responds after a very long moment. "Probably more like I know of you than I know you." followed by another pause.

"As for me," and another pause as he looks away, far away like off into the very depths of everything. He shakes his head yes then as if in silent agreement with some force or thing greater than he.

"As for me girl we aint exactly acquainted yet," and then he trails off as if to test her patience already worn thin.

"So what are you supposed to be then," she asks him with her anger rising to points dangerous and beyond her immediate control as she spits out the rest of the phrase. A fucking haunt for the haunts and never mind how damned strange it sounds.

"Don't you mock me girl," the Ol' Blues Man snaps at her in a short quick bark like counter to her condescending tone. He's flashing his own anger at her dwarfing hers in size and intensity if but for a short moment. Then he's back to his grumbling. A mumbled soliloquy tumbles from his lips. Its part displeasure, a dash of disbelief and a part quarrel with some unseen entity heard in parts and in passing as they seem to be deciding something. She has the uncomfortable feeling it's a decision which most probably concerns her.

"And here I am come to help you," the Ol' Blues Man starts, "but no you don't want any help now do you?"

She hears clearly followed by more mumbling past an unheard phrase but one thing's perfectly clear and comes across as such: ungrateful. She feels a fleeting moment of guilt, almost, or as close as she ever comes to such a feeling.

"Well what's it gonna be then girl," he asks her forgetting for the moment to add his favorite descriptor of damn for her.

"Are you too proud or too mule stubborn to take half a minute to listen to someone who is trying to help your sorry skinny ass along and out of the goodness of my heart here."

"You got something to say just say it old man," she says from her stance right at the end of her run out patience.

"Well damn girl," he says shaking his head, the 'damn girl' now a reflex, a common refrain between the two of them as she seemed able to work on his very last nerve.

"No respect for your elder's then," he says to her, "and here I am trying to help you," his continued refrain though now he's not talking to her anymore. He continues on under his breathe now in a different side conversation and she swears for a moment she can even hear him tsk-tsking her like shame shame shame like a song's refrain in a critique of her behavior.

"Damn girl if you aint nothin' but exasperating," he says, "Trying my patience like you are, damned waste of time is what it is." He pauses sucks in a drag of his cigarette, "Got some things to tell you if you'll quit wasting my time," before he trails off into silence again leaving her to wonder at what he's getting on about.

"Sir," she says as a question trying a different tack this time, trying to shift the conversation around to some advantage for her. She's a little surprised to see how her courtesy actually gives him pause as he seems to reconsider the order of things between them now. It's momentary however.

"Don't you get cute with me girl," he says. He pats his chest before reaching back into his jacket pulling his harp from an inner pocket to casually blow a few notes of the damn chilly fucking tone right up and down her spine the spiteful son of a bitch.

"Do you think you could stop calling me girl," she says in short hard clipped words. Each one is clearly enunciated to demonstrate how her seething anger is, if still under her control. He snorts a hard laugh or it's what she thinks the sound he makes is, though it sounds more like a nasty hard cough or an inhalation of rusty nails scraping against the flesh.

"Oh, now you gonna stand on formalities," he says, "and after all the bragging you been doing bout how one things as good as another," he finishes and now it's her turn to shuffle, to mutter, and then to speak curses under her breathe.

"Guess you got me there old man," she says offering him her patented wicked smile. The old man pauses, seeming to be looking straight through her in such unnerving fashion like once again he's deciding something about her.

Then the most frightening thing she's ever seen in a long time occurs and a small smile cracks the old man's face followed by the heh-heh laugh of his laugh. It sounds like it's been coughed out from somewhere deep within his stained and spotted lungs. For the moment it's clear they're going to be friends, or at least friendly for a little while anyways.

"Sure, what the hell," he says as he shrugs his shoulders. "It's your story after all and makes no never mind to me," though he still sounds a bit grumbly about it, leaving him momentarily lost from whatever it was he'd been about to tell her.

The disconnect stretches out into a very long and exaggerated pause like the Ol' Blues Man has misplaced himself for a moment. It's such a length of time she begins to wonder if the Ol' Blues Man has forgotten her and the reason they find themselves standing here.

"Alright," he starts out but stops short of where he normally inserted his customary girl, though he does leave a small gap there in the sentence. The space is empty and implying all the same.

"There's some things for me to tell you sweetheart."

She's not really appreciating the term sweetheart much more than the previously endearing damn girl either as it drips with heavily sarcastic humoring. But she doesn't interrupt as the Ol' Blues Man continues though she's becoming more than a little tired of all of the unnecessary pauses.

"Now I know you've been out having your fun out knocking about the city deciding things for people and the city, acting like you're its avenger or some such thing. Aint no denying it, I'll respect you less if you do," he says after the singularly longest statement he's ever uttered to her.

A long pause follows as he reaches into his pockets and pulls out the single longest cigarette she's ever seen. He puts it to his lips it with it somehow already lit. He takes a very long drag of it like something out of an old Warner Brothers cartoon draining half of the stick straight to ashes.

"The thing of it is," he says after sucking in another long drag of the cigarette reducing it to mere cartoon ashes and then nothingness. "Despite the mess of a job you do about it, you do actually have the part down," and then he trails off leaving her incredulous how he should choose this spot to leave her hanging.

"Hey," she says flashing a hard stare of displeasure at the old man which has absolutely no effect whatsoever upon him, "how about a little more info there old man."

The Ol' Blues Man stands there impassively with another cigarette smoldering in his hands appearing from she knows not where. He takes another very long drag of cigarette number two. His body language is making it perfectly clear how he's going to move at his own speed irregardless of her desires one way or the other.

"You see the thing of it is sweetheart it's the things you don't know, dontcha know which can rise up and bite you square in the ass," he says finishing cigarette number two in the same fashion as number one.

"And what you don't know, is how you've done riled up the Fates with all of your stomping about and right about when they might have been willing to let things slide if you'd left well enough alone, but no you do the opposite making all this damn noise.

"Insolence is the word for it sweetheart," he says to her and she interrupts him.

"What on earth for," she says in an unjustly persecuted tone of voice. The Old Man is incredulous or at least the expression on his face he's shooting in her direction a look straight from the you've got to be kidding me file.

"Don't give me that who me crap darlin'," he says to her, "you know damn well what for or should." He sucks in a deep breath before launching another lengthy sentence at her.

"Just couldn't stay dead the first time now could you," he says, "and now The Fates have in store for you and your effrontery. Comes a punisher for you, for your hubris of ignoring your death, for not accepting things and going quietly away. Your effrontery for not being dead the first time and for all the damn noise you've been making since. Stomping about so they couldn't ignore you like they'd previously been willing to and this is the mistake made on your part. So The Fates have now done raised a fright to come for you girl and finish things once and for all."

"Yea yea," she says, "and now there'll be hell to pay I suppose," she says her weariness is getting the overall best of her. She's tired of his oblique way of approaching things. Weary of the burden she's been weighed down with of late and it creeps into her tone.

"Well great, just fucking great," she says looking away from him for a moment. Her cynicism is rising at the same rate as her exasperation.

"Look Old Man I've got enough troubles already without borrowing any of yours, so you can kindly pack 'em up and piss off to parts unknown thank you very much." She finishes her retort with a scoffing breath out over her shoulder in a look away moment.

The Blues Man looks at her with an expression somewhere between incredulous, sadness and a strange admiration for her nonchalance in the face of such things. He expresses this in his cough laugh escaping past his lips, but it's a prelude to his anger soon to be expressed.

"Damn it all girl," the Ol' Blues Man says returning back to the use of girl. "This aint no joke girl, aint speaking of no such quaint a thing like hell to pay here, not when you have beings even the gods fear taking notice of you!"

"Even you Old Man," she says biting deep, "even you're afraid of them."

He straightens up his whole person ramrod straight and purses his lips. He straightens his clothes and mumbles something about her not taking this seriously.

"You don't want to listen to me it's alright, aint no never mind to me," he retorts loudly.

He then nods his head as his hands return themselves to absently patting his pockets and settling for a moment. It's clear he's reached a conclusion about her which he doesn't share before he spins in a twisty motion. The man disappears in a turning whisp of color and smoke and then nothing. The Ol' Blues Man is straight up, clear and gone into the thin air leaving her suddenly alone.

Damn that spooky shit leaving a chill running up and down her spine. An accomplishment most unnerving which she badly wants to shake off. But damn if this encounter didn't have her spooked even if she was loath to admit to even the idea of it. She somehow left with the unshakable understanding how this was not to be the last of these encounters with the strange old man.

She's beginning to feel sour about the whole damn thing even without the looming specter of the warning the Old Man had passed along to her. She could feel it pressing down on her in a sick mimicry of the approaching storm. It's almost enough for her to question her sanity were it not already an asked and answered form of a thought process or a difference between sane or not could be noticed or told.

She steps off in the opposite direction down to the lower Quarter and over to Molly's to get some whiskey, some bourbon and whatever else she can until these thoughts are drowned away.

Saudade

A long sigh escapes her. One much longer than she'd thought to expel. A sign of how perhaps things are a bit deeper embedded than she'd previously gauged them to be, plumbing the depths for rock bottom of her malaise. Damn but she wishes this were a drunk tonight, as opposed to these more sober thoughts. She prefers the prettier look from within the ambered liquor as opposed to the starkness of the reality, or unreality or whatever the hell this is for her in the in-between.

The contending cacophony of the ever nearing thunder of Isaac and his play partner The Terrible Fright are combining with the faint lingering melancholic sound of the Blues Man's harp to deafen her. They cling to her, seeming to demand more and more of her attention or are simply becoming harder and harder to ignore. They add each in their own way to her deepening feeling of dread and depression. This strange condition she seemed to remember from a place far off somewhere as being called saudade or perhaps it's the pull of the river and its patron still calling to her.

She's feeling reflective for a change. Wandering lost within her own thoughts for reasons which are solidly beyond her. She's simply another lost soul wandering in the city of night milling with the rest of the crowd, the plethora of creatures of the night. The not so cryptic warning of the Ol' Blues Man being made real with the first bands of the storm were reason enough for her to do some thinking and searching out of a counter viewpoint. This will be her retroactive excuse later for where she finds herself presently.

She's arrived along the alley next to the mass of oldest basilica in North America and looks up at its

edifice. She's not certain why she should find herself here
of all places except for the quiet beauty and peacefulness
which can be found within its confines. The cathedral has
excellent air conditioning and is a nice escape from the
city's heat. It's certainly not because she's expecting much
of anything else to be found here. She steps through the
doors without harm as she has so many times before.

Sacred ground has never been an impediment to
her, has never offered any resistance to her. And another
myth is disproven to an initial disappointment though
she's glad of it in the long run. It offered her safe place to
rest at night, like all the other creatures of the night, away
from the prying eyes of the world. Besides, this ground
isn't sacred cause of any single god confined within the
walls of the cathedral or loose out in the world at large
either. If there is any sacredness here, it has much more
to do with all of the blood stained into the grounds
before the cathedral. Executioner's ground oft used in the
fifty years or so of the French period of the city's history.

She sits on the right side of the cathedral without
any particular agenda and yet her presence seems to

disturb those gathered. It does so in a fairly wide swath judging by the people who hurry from the cathedral while making the sign of the cross as they pass near her spot. She pays the machinations no mind. It seems to be so much over exaggerated reaction to her presence. Yet, the longer she stays the more she notices the stares, the avoidance, and the application of the self-blessing and it irks her and not bothering anybody actively. She's merely taking up space on the left hand side of god before she remembers how it's not as coveted a spot as previously advertised.

She can feel the approach of someone with the rise of the hairs on the back of her neck. She presumes this person to be a priest and is annoyed at the intrusion, at the selection of her person for confrontation as she adopts a 'what now' attitude.

"Well padre," she says as the priest nears in his approach to her. It gives him a momentary pause to wonder how she could have known he was there when he was coming up on her from behind her. Where she theoretically shouldn't, and presumably couldn't know he was there. Not something which should ever be done to any of her type or kind, not if you had a lick of sense that is. The call for self-preservation sounding like every warning bell a person could have.

"This is a house of god he tells her," as if it wasn't previously painfully obvious what with the giant cross over the altar and center stage as it were. Their savior affixed to so he might look down over his subjects, "and we expect a certain amount of decorum within these walls."

"Forgive me padre," she says feeling like she's channeling Clancy Brown for a moment. She certainly feels like a monster and the one everyone should rightly be afraid of house of god or not.

"But I've come for confession padre," she says disingenuously over her wicked little smile but the priest aint buying it either. This is much to his credit, though it's a rather transparent form of pure bullshit on her part.

The priest is still visibly upset his face turning red all the way up to his ears as he sputters out to her the accusation of blasphemer to which she chuckles a little further on about.

"Well padre, she says, you don't know the half of it on that one," and there she giggles in a decidedly unmonstrous kind of way while she stands to stretch. She moves in a quick dart to whisper boo in his ear which causes him to jump. She moves on past him into the aisle of the cathedral making her way out towards the doors as the new arrivals push forward mostly to get away from her.

"Affront to god," she says over her shoulder as she leaves, "can you really be so sure padre? Remember padre how we are all of us god's creatures," followed by her wicked little laugh as she's enjoying herself.

"Every one of us," she says as a finale before she turns and spins on her heel to the rear of the church. She pauses to look back at him while she blows him a kiss from the narthex of the church before spinning out in a burst through the front doors and into the daylight with more of her wicked little laugh.

The priest performs the signum crucis trying to suppress the knowledge which goes with his shudder from this very close encounter with one of god's more frightening creatures. Creatures usually spoken of as warnings to those who stray from the line of doctrine or faith and never mind how his faith did not generally account for these types of supernatural things.

Well, that was a singularly bad idea on her part, she thinks in a mild admonishment. She steps off from the cathedral to stop on the pavers in front of the old basilica. She stands on the old executioner's ground feeling all of the haunts which the old blood promises and draws up into the world. The blood doesn't smell like old blood to her though. It still smells somewhat fresh to her, slick and coppery yet and she deeply breathes in its essence almost able to sense and see the scenes which this near ancient ground has born witness to from over the centuries before the basilica ever had a stone set down over the sacred ground.

She walks out from the park which lies there now in the modern day. A little stumble to her step and a laugh at the irony of appearing like a drunk as she tilts her crooked way away from the square in an alteration to her usual course towards the river. She heads through the Quarter in atypical fashion, towards Rampart and to the graveyard there. She enters St. Louis Number One feeling compelled to pay homage to Marie Laveau, the true protectress of the city. She places a coin at Marie's tomb, the first one right inside the gates. She'll place coins before the other two tombs before she leaves as well, no sense in even unintentional offense. The sounds of the Quarter and the city in general are distant. They seem unable to cross the walls which surround St. Louis Number One which keep both the city out and the haunts within.

As she leaves the graveyard her fingertips brush against the high white walls to tantalize her with their hinted textures. She can hear the river calling to her, coaxing her to its shores, where she can stare out across the waters and ease her burdens in the depths of his infinite patience. The river, her unintentional last choice when it should've been the first place for her to seek out, but maybe she'd wanted to avoid the obviousness bordering on cliché of the choice. She shrugs her shoulders at the entire thought process as she steps off in a straight line towards the cliché.

She wends her way down towards the edge of the waters of the ancient river to sit on a bench near her favorite spot on the small levee overlooking the river. Her legs swing freely beneath the bench in a purely childlike joy which make it so much more enjoyable. She has the bench and most of the walk to herself, except for a few strays. The moon's reflection shimmers in the always moving water and though she seems unaware of it, she's deciding something or coming closer to it as she looks out over the river.

Tonight should be a night for hunting, for her to be out prowling in the darkness with the other night creatures going bump, but she's too strangely distracted by the relentless ticking of a clock. She cannot seem to stop hearing the ticking. She uncomfortably realizes how the exception is when the Ol' Blues Man plays his harp. It's an uncomfortable thought, as it further aids her general feeling of restlessness, a feeling of being out of time despite the constant ticking pestering her like the damn croc ever after Captain Hook.

Timeless. But what's the point of it? She can't help but wonder when she's standing outside of time watching as the city's already moving on and becoming slowly unrecognizable to her. Adding to her general state of melancholia, her wondering about the commonality of this affliction amongst her fellow dead or if it applies just to her.

She's half hoping to see the Man of the Waters but she's in the wrong spot for it. It's too bright along this thin stretch of park against the river. She needs to move farther down river to the Governor Nicholls Wharf at a minimum, if not farther, if she should really hope to see him. It's just as well tonight, for she was at the wrong hour for any proper interaction and she didn't have any story to tell him as an offering or otherwise. It was simply bad form to call on one such as him without anything to offer in reciprocation. Disrespectful to waste any eternal's time she knew and a particular quirk of his which she'd never quite gotten used to. He absolutely hated so to waste his time and he certainly wouldn't appreciate the interruption.

She never wanted to irk him when he was one of the few haunts and bumps here in the city which would talk to her at all. Tonight she's feeling a bit reckless though, and is deciding to hang all of it and push her luck. She calls to him but The Man of The Waters doesn't respond to her. She hadn't expected he would when it was all wrong this choice. It was too early in the night, too far from the proverbial witching hour of midnight or farther into the night as is their usual pattern and she so far away from their usual spot with nothing but a series of excuses for calling upon the Man of the Waters. It leaves her to wonder what the hell she was thinking about or hoping to accomplish.

There are only apologies to offer now to the aforementioned waste of his time. She pours them out in quick profusion grateful for the fact of The Man of The

Water's infinite patience. He'll wait forever for her if it's what's called for. He's in no hurry after all. There's a comfort there for her with this knowledge and in her decision now made. The time will come is ever so close now, so close as to be without measure, to even see the small distance lying between them though but not for much longer.

For one more day she resists the call of the river but it's a near thing. A call too close for differentiation or definition and, such a very near thing, followed by a very long sigh she wanted to disown but couldn't escape. She'll content herself instead with the proximity of his shores from the bench she currently occupies with one leg underneath her the other swinging free. Her hands stay in her pockets and the waters still calling for her with a melancholic tune which matches her current melancholic attitude. The song briefly follows a little too closely to the same mournful tune which usually preceded the Ol' Blues Man. It's throwing a chill up and down her damn spine causing her to almost look over her shoulder half expecting him to be there.

She dawdles, delaying her departure, the joys of having no particular place to go or be outside of the Terrible Fright. The Fright was coming for her so all she had to do was wait for his arrival like an anxious host on a delayed guest. She sits for a very long time looking out over the river wishing for more peaceful moments like this one, unaware for a tick of the time passing. She's waiting on some kind of something to propel her to action though nothing particularly compelling has crossed her mind when she finally rises to leave her favorite spot.

When she stands she spots something underneath the bench. She can hear a flipping sound in the breeze and she kneels down to look beneath the bench where she sees a small paperback book there, its pages flapping unhappily. The book seems abandoned or lost and as she stoops down to pick it up finding the book to be instantly familiar to her touch. It's sending what passes for chills in her present condition through her body. It's a peculiar phenomenon not previously experienced in this in-between life of hers such as it is. The strangely familiar book calls to her saying come claim me I'm your property after all. She picks the book up and reveals itself to be a worn book which she surprisingly does actually recognize.

It's the same book she used to have way back when. The same one which persistently fell open to page 126 and 127 due to its broken spine. A pretense it has given up with its first half gone missing now which she thinks, simply won't do. It bothers her how it should have traveled this far back to her only to be incomplete. She rummages through the pile of debris under the bench for its other portions working to uncover them. She's feeling the better for it when she finds the other part allowing her to be able to complete the book such as it was or ever was going to be. Near back to when it had first been found so long ago like a talisman or a relic or, most likely, by pure ironic chance.

She's surprised to see the book. Her copy of the old Stoker book thought lost with the misadventures of the foolish northern woman who'd thought to take possession of her things a few years back. The book was still smeared with mud, a stale earth smell within its torn and frayed pages and bloated from the waters it had taken in. Its spine is broken in more than one place now, though it still retains its predilection or perhaps affinity for page 126 and 127 and its strongly emphasized quote underlined in red by the previous owner. She laughs at the book's return to her and wonders at the many mysteries of the universe which should cause it to find its way back to her at this late date.

Most likely though there's no rhyme or reason for it, just some random generator of chance or some such other mechanism of the universe and is no never mind anyway. Some things are not meant to be understood she knows as she pockets the book glad to have found it. Reclaimed, the better word for the feeling of lost property returned and making her whole. Though somehow the thought doesn't feel exactly right either, seems to be a bit off the point and yet somehow correct all the same. It's an uncomfortable thought which could plague and perplex her if she were to allow it to do so as she attempts to shake it from her mind.

She steps off into the dark, one hand still resting within her pocket clutched loosely around the Stoker book. She finds a strange comfort in its presence there deep in a pocket inside of her beat to hell seen better days leather jacket. She's already forgotten her casual casting over the waters of the river the river's ancient name. She never thought to consider how the book had been provided as a sign of the Man of the Waters having heard her. He provides her this boon as a form of small comfort in the face of the storm and The Terrible Fright closing in on the city.

The Terrible Fright

The first booms of The Terrible Fright arrive in the cusp of early evening on a Tuesday echoing out across the city and are hard enough for her to feel in the soles of her feet on the pavement of the city. They knock her out of her normal stride as much as out of her general malaise with the fearful reminder how she has little time left on her own personal clock. The Fates are already measuring off her thread of life with scissors sharp as they take up looking for the right proper place to make the snip.

It's a shock to feel the Ol' Blues Man's warning now made real. How it's come to life with a quick moment of regret she'd not allotted more time for the Blues Man to finish telling her everything he might have followed by a quick flash of defiance. What more could the old man have really told her? What more could he have said which would have changed the outcome? If the outcome has been decreed by, as he'd said, by beings which even the gods fear, then what chance did an abjuration such as she herself have.

She feels something she's not felt in a very long time. A time longer than the years passed and an excellent example of actual physical world time and the way it's calculated, but mostly gone untallied in the in-between place she was a solid inhabitant of. She felt fear, real fear. It lay in a thin fragile layer beneath her typical state of mind of anger. Here, at last, she has a place to vent her rage upon, a cause cèlébre to rally her rage upon and then against. What has she done and to whom to have earned this enmity? To have someone set this Terrible Fright against her?

Has she given such offense then simply by her still being here in this weird little carved out space she calls the in-between? This simple act of being is such the crime then. So criminal as to have offended the gods where they feel compelled to come down with more punishment for her in the form of the Terrible Fright.

The Ol' Blues Man had told her how it was more about her inability to stay down, as he'd so eloquently put it which had drawn the ire of the Fates. How it was her *being* in this case, which was crime enough, to justify the response coming soon.

The god's collective eyes previously and seemingly forever turned away from her before now. Before her existence had rubbed their collective noses with the persistent reminder how even gods can make mistakes. How even the gods are flawed and even their infinite plans can go awry. And this, the greatest offence she has inadvertently offered. Living proof, as it were, of the mistake made and most importantly; there for the entire world to see.

Thus is the punishment offered to her without any act of contrition available to her. There's no penance to complete which might bring the benevolent notice of the god's back to her.

The Terrible Fright minds not any of her reasoning and still comes for her in excellent disguise, tactic and plan. He comes as a storm once more to these ever battered shores and she at her weakest moment and he with all intentions of exploiting it as best can be done and much to her detriment.

The Terrible Fright rides in on the winds of the storm called Isaac by coincidence or, more likely, in conspiratorial cooperation with the storm as they share in its projected menace and promises of doom. The Terrible Fright demands to be faced. The assault on the city's defenses begins. They're designed to overwhelm or to strike when most had gotten the hell out of the way by leaving town and the rest had their heads down due to the approaching storm.

She can feel the pressure of the Terrible Fright's existence within the storm. Even at whatever distance this is from him to her and can almost sense the single minded malevolence. It damn near seethes off of him in frightening quality and quantity.

The Terrible Fright comes looking for her from parts unknown to settle the scores of very old gods who are, in very ungodlike fashion, jealous over having been forgotten or worse, and in her particular case, ignored. She'd been told once, hell probably more than once, how she should be careful about raising a scare. All of the noise she'd been making stomping around the older parts of the city like she'd been doing over the last seven plus years. Her merry misadventures and deeds across the city serving to call forth the Fright.

The ancient names and descriptions of the Terrible Fright read like a litany of synonyms for every kind of bad which has ever been visited upon mankind. The monolithic horror, the black hearted bastard, the heartless killing machine are all based upon him. But he is no fiction, he is altogether very real and dispatched by as a scourge to cleanse the world of that which displeases those most displeased.

The Terrible Fright's a grim bastard of the first order looking for her and not being too terribly subtle about it either. A brute come a knockin' when he comes ashore and moves inland to hit the city from the south and west as his principle method of movement in typical storm fashion. The behemoth is as dull witted as befits a blunt instrument. It wouldn't seem too particularly hard to find her, though she might not be advertising her presence, she certainly wasn't exactly inconspicuous either. And still he pounds about the Quarter and anything or one in his way for good measure too. Crashing about and terrorizing the locals without necessity or cause as they've little to do with her or the dispute. The monster is seeking her out if only she would oblige him and soonest.

The first bands of the storm reach into the heart of the city and include his first lashings at her which knock her clean off of her feet. She's shocked and terribly, deeply, frightened by his might not knowing how it is she could stand against a creature which the Fates have set against her.

Damn hell, but that was a wallop of one slamming hit delivered with such obvious strength behind the power of a humongous hand. The blow trying hard to knock her straight off to the land of the dead and never mind how this is where she quite rightly belongs. Amazing, frightful strength and the Fright still a day away from her and this is the very farthest his reach stretches. It is one helluva introduction he hath wrought even at this distance for their first encounter.

It was a clever maneuver of The Fates to have chosen the anniversary for this strike of theirs. Getting in such close proximity and parallel to the date. Down to or near enough to the actual minute to mark another happy anniversary. This is when she's weakest, something about it being her creation day she understands but not the why of it. It had never really troubled her before though it was certainly feeling fairly important in the here and now.

She didn't feel much like applauding them from where she lies sprawled on the pavers of her city. The Terrible Fright is here in her city if slightly ahead of the main force of the storm proper. The Fright is eager for her, eager for a piece of her and anything else which gets in his way. Maximum damage his pleasure.

She crab crawls away from the Fright in the lull of the moment creating some space between the two of them. She doesn't ask herself why he pauses here, she's simply grateful for it until the Ol' Blues Man appears right over the shoulder of The Terrible Fright. He wears a way too wide a grin on his face enjoying the spectacle way too much.

"Comes the scourge girl to wipe your skinny ass from off the planet," he yells to her his voice still able to carry somehow through the storm.

"Your Fate comes to claim you girl, to reset the balance of things and all because you couldn't leave well enough alone and stay dead."

This is followed by more of his wide grin for her, all the more frightening as it sends shivers up and down her damn spine. Not for long though fortunately, with

The Terrible Fright blotting out most everything else of any concern and commanding all of her attention.

The second punch arrives much as the first as she's back on her feet standing, though, again, not for long. She's thrown back on her ass in the streets drenched now from the rains rain and the pools gathered from the curbs outward. She's looking like the proverbial drowned rat though she could really do without the iconography. She hurts everywhere and she can taste fear as the Terrible Fright waits for her to stand for whatever reasoning which exists within his impenetrable hide.

"Stay down," the Ol' Blues Man taunts her as the Fright waits once more for her to stand so he can knock her down once more.

"Stay down girl it's not too late girl," he continues, "give in and accept your fate," he finishes telling her and she'd really rather he'd go and whisper in someone else's ear for a change.

She flops over from her back into the classic push up position. She executes the maneuver while drawing her knees beneath her as she catches her breath. She then straightens upright to rock back on her heels with her face to the skies and the pounding rain. She lets out a defiant scream or one of frustration but hopefully not her death rattle. She stands and turns back round to face the Terrible Fright while ignoring the Ol' Blues Man's evil grin. The Fright stands before her without any expression at all.

"Too bad you couldn't have stayed down," the Ol' Blues Man somehow manages to say to her right into her ear like he's on her shoulder. He then disappears in the same damn creepy wisp of eerie mist with the fading sound of his harp still rattling through the pounding rain.

She faces The Fright unable to get a good look at him through the storm which grows with intensity with each passing moment. She guesses this is the end of round one between them. She's trying hard not to think of how much she's straight fucked here if this is but a sampling of the power of The Terrible Fright.

The Terrible Fright's moves in on her to the sound of an invisible bell signaling round two and falls upon her with a barrage of punches like sledge hammer blows. They fall like the rain without cessation or even the promise of it. The pure destructive force of a nature which could wipe her from the planet and cleanse her from this mortal palette. The Fright provides maximum punishment in even the glancing blows though there aren't many of those offered. Each punch seems to find their mark and she doesn't know how much more of this she can take.

Dishearteningly, The Terrible Fright seems unaffected from the battle so far. He doesn't even seem winded or marked from their initial introductions. His already great strength increases as he draws power direct from the storm raging away. He keeps after her no matter how fast or far she scrambles away from him. He stays blessedly unaware how she's drawing him away from the city proper and down to the river in her typical and so ingrained as to be subconscious pattern. The Terrible Fright keeps to his glacially purposeful and intimidating pace bringing his full force to bear against her. He's bearing down with his obelisk like mass threatening to crush and leave her like a stain upon the pavers of the city.

She instinctively sought the river, drawing the Terrible Fright down with her towards the Governor Nicholls Wharf and farther. The Terrible Fright continues to hammer away at her with freight train packed punches. She soon cries out in terror and pain as her desperation threatens to turn to despair.

She knows she's soon to be defeated by the thundering monster leaving his undefeated streak intact and unblemished unless, by some minor miracle, she can come up with some strategy to defeat him. File it under major miracle please as she had no idea in hell how to possibly end The Fright who'd not shown even the slightest inclination of any form of weakness or anything else which she might exploit, not even a little bit.

The Terrible Fright's last punch descends as she scrabbles on the pavers near her bend of the river. In her last prescient act before The Fright completes the action she finally calls out to The Man of the Waters to offer herself to him and his benevolence. She finishes right as a punch lands and knocks her clear to silence before she can know if The Man of the Waters has heard her call.

The Man of the Waters

She slips gratefully into the blackness, thankful for the reprieve and a pronounced calm unlike anything else she's ever previously encountered which included her first death. She knows the Terrible Fright and his conspirator Isaac still lash the city and her physical form with the intention of reducing her back to nothingness and she's strangely glad it might finally be done for her.

Her slow slip into the blackness would bring more comfort to her if it didn't also dredge up so many uncomfortable and thought forgotten things from her first death. Her death then rise as a haunt amongst the chaos and damage caused by Miss K seven years ago and the unpleasantness which followed in its waning.

Seven for the devil, but seven is also a power number with many meanings and representations throughout the world. Seven is a god in one world and a legendary monster in another further and a part of the fuel behind The Fright and whether a god or a monster was mostly a moot point with The Fright certainly here.

She'd been too caught up in the number of this anniversary as some form of fateful mark and had almost missed an important detail. She'd laugh at it if she could, the idiom which came to immediate mind of the 'devil in the details.' The Fates had loosed a monster upon her in the form of The Terrible Fright with the storm as his source of strength. This then the detail missed, as the nature of storms is such that no matter their size or strength, they always, eventually, pass on.

She sinks further into the blackness. She's less troubled by things despite the clarity recently received holding on to her one, and very last, thought. She still doesn't know if The Man of the Waters has heard her call before full blackness takes her.

The waters of the river begin to stir beneath the storm and in direct defiance of the courses it tries to push it in. Ripples from deep within the ancient, ever moving, river rise silently to take no specifically discernable shape, other than to be clearly above the regular rise of the river in its typical course. This mass reaches out to her and as it does, it eventually takes on the shape of a man or human shape at a minimum offering her a hand to hold on to.

The river calls to her like it doesn't already have her full attention somehow but she'll forgive the river of all kinds of things. It is a river after all and must find the transmutation an impossible task to complete on scale alone. The river tells her how, contrary to the Ol' Blues Man's words, she's not actually in debt to the Fates solely or more precisely, she doesn't have to ascribe to their version of events. She doesn't have to accept what has been laid out for her, he tells her. There are other options for her if she should so choose it.

My sweet lovely, he communicates in a whisper inside her mind as he tells her fantastical tales from what mortal men would call myth or legend.

Specifically the one option he's providing to her to now to join with the river. Accept his proposal and come into the river and become an eternal with him. She was not raised a haunt or any other thing after all. She's the protector of the city and that much she'd gotten correct. She's in transition and coming into the fullness of her own powers if she could only see it, and understand it. If she should accept his offer, she will fulfill another destiny entirely without abandoning her role as protector of the city.

Accept him, be his bride, and take on the mantle. Become what she's so richly earned over the years each time she'd returned to him. Accept his offer and he will complete her transition. He will make her a river goddess, a battle goddess in full Celtic.

Be his goddess, his champion and companion and all of the power of the river will be hers to harness, to command, but only if she accepts what he proposes.

Join me my lovely he says to her his voice deep, warm, and calm, filled with all of the languages which have ever been spoken over him over the many, many years of his existence.

Embrace me my sweetly.
Become eternal my love.
Become his bride and be remade his offer to her
Become his bride and be reborn as the river's goddess in the Celtic tradition.
Become, he says to her as the form slowly dissolves back into the waters which had made it and the full thundering and fury of the storm returns to her ears.

The Hard Rain

The full thundering and fury of the storm rings in her ears in concert with the continued hammering blows from The Fright's still standing over her she spits up a mouthful of rain into his face. She follows with her death rattle, turned now to a battle cry, as she crawls from underneath the hammering to rises up against the protest of her aching bones.

She stands despite all protests from every outpost and extremity of her person with pain coursing through her. She's disheveled and her clothes torn even more though most surprisingly blood is trickling from her nose, her scalp and other parts to rivulet down her body. The blood pools in unnatural places sticky and viscous. It continues moving ever downward to squish in her shoes and mark the pavement wherever she steps leaving blood on the pavers including an outline on the sidewalk where she'd just lain splayed out like a corpse.

A small separation has opened up between them now as The Fright pauses for whatever reason, giving her a moment to note how a crowd has gathered all about the edges of their battle. The crowd formed from all of the cities' ghosts and long dead combined with most if not all of the cities other supernatural haunts. She wonders how the betting's going as round three begins. It has been admittedly, so far, a one sided fight despite how it might be spun as a battle of titans but only from a mythical post tense standpoint.

The nature of storms is how they must always, eventually, pass on. It's an important piece of information pulled from out of her blackness. The key to defeating the Terrible Fright is the same as any storm and twofold: wait it out, *withstand* it and him. *Withstand* The Terrible

Fright. *Withstand* him, because The Fright has a limited time to defeat her. A mistake of necessity from The Fates as they dared not leave something so powerful out and about the place lest it one day, someday, might turn against them. Their own fear is their undoing as long as she can *withstand* it.

She must make a stand against The Terrible Fright to defeat him. She must take whatever punishment The Terrible Fright can dish out until his strength is diminished and he moves onward inland in defeat. His strength played out, his size diminished. This then is the second mistake made by The Fates in the choosing of The Fright as champion to face her. It's a grievous error to dish out pain to her when she's a creature whose very nature is to take pain and turn it into sustenance.

The key in defeating The Fright is with her indefatigableness. To still stand no matter what he dishes out against her. To trust in the strength and resiliency from a city she's sworn herself to. The city still here on the river standing against all the storms, still stubbornly here despite odds given and stacked mostly against her entire obstinate existence.

Beneath the continued onslaught of The Fright she *withstands* knowing there is nothing he can do which can ever erase her from these shores, as long as she has the city and the river to gird her efforts. She grits her teeth as she calls on every reserve of internal strength she has and turns it into a shield to take the continuous hammering blows from The Terrible Fright. With her feet on the ground and the river to her left, she has reserves aplenty for as long as she should wish to *withstand* the Terrible Fright's might.

The Terrible Fright draws from the rage and power of the storm. From the rains and the wind but storms eventually pass on, as they must, while she has the stubborn permanence of the city coupled with the timelessness of The Man of The Waters and the river which has formed and defined this city's existence across the ages. She must simply *withstand* The Fright and still be here like the city has for all of her long centuries in defiance against The Fright.

The Man of The Waters had said to her accept me and you shall rise my bride in your rightful guise as my beloved, as my goddess in the proudest Celtic tradition. Celtic tales told of river goddess' who act also as battle goddess' and who do not shy from the taste of battle or bloodshed.

She'd said yes of course. Her last words before the blackness had claimed her and now she stood here betrothed to The Man of the Waters. She could feel the promise of his eternal strength rising up in her with her full evolution now as a Celtic battle goddess come to meet the enemy.

The Terrible Fright continues battering her, still throwing punches like cannon shots hammering down in an echo of the frequency and fury while the storm rails about and against the city. The winds and rains of the storm match the strength of the raging Fright as he draws more strength from the force of the waters lashing against the city, from the power of the ripping wind which howls its rage turning into his battle cry. His fists rise up and strike her again and again with renewed force and pressure driving her almost to her knees. More blood falls from her turning from trickles to an outright flow from her eyes, her ears, nose and mouth.

And, no lie, she's a little disappointed initially as there seems to be no immediate effect or benefit from her little bargain with The Man of the Water until after surviving the barrage of punches received from The Terrible Fright. She notes how the fight now feels significantly different for both of them and understands what is needed now, and is momentarily sorry she ever doubted The Man of the Waters and his promise, his sincerity.

For the first time The Terrible Fright hesitates, has doubt and she smiles her crooked trademarked wicked smile as she understands now. She understands the necessity of knocking the ordinary off of her to complete the remake of her character into the fullness of a Celtic battle goddess for this is how a battle goddess is made: in blood and pain.

She smiles through each and every punch from The Terrible Fright as he works away the layers of her ordinariness. She endures the onslaught as each strike strips her of who she was and reveals another piece of her new incarnation as a Celtic battle goddess. Her laugh fills the ears of The Fright without slowing his assault. Her laughter somehow echoes past him and across the pavers and walls of the city as she revels in her rebirth. She can feel the strength of The Man of The Waters as a bulwark to her own strength. She even feels the earned begrudging approval of the city's principle protectress, her graveyard homage to Marie paying dividends for her.

Withstand, and she does for endless hours smiling all the length of them. The Fright pays her no mind as he continues his assault, standing over her somehow but not as strong or as fast as before.

The Terrible Fright grows progressively weaker with each hour that passes and still she stands before him unreduced. They can both feel the shift of the storm as it bounces away from the city and farther west. The Terrible Fright looks up to the thinning sky and almost seems sad for a moment. The Fright a tragic figure now with the loss of his unbeaten streak. His chin sits on his chest and his shoulders are shrunk in for a moment. He shrugs his massive shoulders, he lifts his head and he nods an okay at her. It is a mark of respect and understanding before he turns a step away to vanish into the storm.

The battle ends in disturbing quiet with the departure of The Terrible Fright. She teeters up off of her heels and back onto her toes threatening to fall, to keel over a more appropriate descriptor for her current condition. Her shoulders hunched inwards and her balance thrown off, disorientated, dizzy and paler than she'd ever been before. Her weight shifts and she has her heels back under her once more and is, let's be generous, standing on her own two feet. Though like an old, old joke, not for long.

She's flat damned exhausted and teetering in the absence of The Fright. The rain starts to abate, the wind slows, and the waves return to their normal heights. Her wicked smile is diminished to a straight line as she feels all of the pain from the epic battle which she'd been able to ignore in the midst the conflict, all returned to her now with its passing.

The storm has moved on taking the Fright with because even a hard rain, a deluge cannot fall forever. The rain has to stop sometime to allow the unfailing sun to break through to the city, to shine down upon her streets. The steam will soon rise up to quickly dry up the traces left on the sidewalks and pavement.

But that's for another day. A day she'll not see. She won't make it past the next dark of night. She looks up as the clouds part for a moment, as is fashionably called for in any epic told and can feel the benevolence of the moon goddess above who seems to smile her light down upon her.

Sighs

Staggered, she falters near collapse from the epic fight with The Terrible Fright. Every last ounce of her strength had been used to stand in disbelief at the ability to do so. She did not know how much longer it should last but suspects it is but mere moments. She succumbs in a fall to her knees, bent forward as some sound or piece of her tries to escape from her lips or body to retch on the pavement in a long dangled, unbroken line of spit and blood from her mouth. If she could cry, she would. So much pain, too much pain, unwelcome and unfelt for years gone by now. Perhaps it's her time running out past its expiration date and The Fates have succeeded in their quest despite the passing of The Terrible Fright.

She rejects the notion as she gets up and returns to her usual spot by the river to extract a return upon a promise made. To say yes once more to The Man of the Waters and accept his embrace and be his bride.

She'll thwart The Fates with a choice for herself once and everyone else can go hang. She then steers a more or less straight course to The Man of the Waters so they can have their wedding night. One last slip away into the pleasant deep warm embrace of one who'd called her beloved.

"Damn if you aint a sight baby girl," the Ol' Blues Man says so softly, almost under his breath as if he too is put off by what has been wrought by the storm and The Terrible Fright.

She's mildly surprised to see him here appearing for once without his tell-tale distinctive harmonica sound to announce him.

"You should see the other guy," she says to him and the Ol' Blues Man actually looks over his shoulder briefly giving her a quick chuckle which aches all the way throughout her body, bones and soul and everything.

He turns back to her and though she knows she's wrong, she swears for a moment there the old man had actual genuine concern for her, as disconcerting an idea as it is. He covers this with the heh-heh of his distinctive and strange cough laugh before drifting off away from her for a moment.

"What do you want old man," she finally asks after too long a silence has passed. She feels for the first time since this whole thing started like she's actually pressed for time but dammit she's exhausted and all she wants to do is lie down for a hundred years or more.

"Aint about my wants there baby girl." He says. More cryptic nonsense from the Ol' Blues Man as he surveys her battered person from head to toe and back again.

"It aint never been about what I want at all there baby girl," he finishes followed by the big unsettling smile of his. Straight damn creepy is what it is.

Another long moment drags out too far and she can feel the press of time against her. She knows there's not much more left for her and she needs to hurry to finish the way she prefers, before the choice is no longer hers to make anymore.

"Thought we'd settled that girl shit there old man," she snaps back at him having misheard his affectation because she's still fairly seriously pissed off and in too much damn pain to even pretend to be polite.

"Yea yeah," The Ol' Blues Man says tapping out an impossibly long streak of ash from an equally impossibly long cigarette. He raises the long cigarette back to his lips to take a long drag of it, letting the smoke fill his lungs.

"Slipped my mind," he finishes saying before he trails off looking far afield but without any more words to indicate whatever it was he'd wanted in this particular moment. He turns to her and smiles once more followed by the cough- laugh of his still threatening to dislodge a lung or at least sounding capable of such an act.

"Thwarted the Fates and become what you were supposed to be," more crypticness from him but she's too damn tired to care much even if she has one more question for him.

"Whose side are you on anyway," she asks and he looks at her and again with that laugh of his leaving the hairs on the back of her neck standing up.

"Sometimes we don't get the answers we seek," he says. "Sometimes things turn out as they must need to be, with a little prompting along the way so they can be finished now."

"Sonnaofabitch," she says it loudly though she'd meant it to be said under her breath. She understood now, how the Ol' Blues Man means more than one thing in his use of the word finished and his role in all of this becomes very clear to her causing her to repeat her use of the term, sonnaofabitch.

"Yea yeah," he tells her, "not much left to say nor the time for it, is there now baby girl," and she scowls unhappy with the exchange, knowing there isn't much better she can get from him.

"You saved the city and have earned your rest, so go on now," the Ol' Blues Man says to her, "go on he's waiting on you baby girl. I'll play you a tune to carry you home baby girl," he finishes and she nods her head in agreement as she turns away from to face back to the river.

She turns down the banks and is but a step away from the river when she remembers one last thing she has to do and she quickly scrambles back up the bank to the bench. She stops and straightens up for a moment.

She pats the pockets of her tattered beat to hell jacket in a search for the book she'd placed there like a talisman or lucky charm or perhaps bad penny was a better choice for this object which kept appearing through the thread of her story. A story very near its end now. She holds the book in her hands drawing comfort from its beat to hell pages feeling a kinship with it as she opens it, the first time she has. Her fingers find page 126 and 127 of course and the quote so strongly emphasized in underwritten red ink. She reads the highlighted line and understands now, how she is under the beneficent grace emphasized there.

She stands for a moment looking out over the city, the book in her hand at her hip as she makes one last decision to leave the book behind. She places the old Stoker book on the bench overlooking the waters knowing it belongs here. She leaves it to the city in a nice bit of circular completion and then she sighs, a very long sigh. She feels done and realizes she doesn't want to wait any longer.

"Ready," the Ol' Blues Man asks her. It's an unexpected courtesy and she simply nods her head as she leaves her bench with the book on it open and fluttering in the wind. She steps off the sidewalk and down the embankment as he wets his lips, his harp in hand and at the ready.

She's at the river's edge with the toes of her boots touching the water. The Blues Man's song finds her ears and fills them with a pleasant if bittersweet tune of sleep. A lullaby, just for her as she begins her slip beneath the waters.

Mississippi Queen

The Man of the Waters is calling to her, coaxing her with his deep warm tones ever inviting, his patience still and ever present as he waits for her beneath the waters eternal and enduring. She sighs, a long deep sigh as she imagines for a moment the peacefulness he promises her in his ceaseless and uncaring continuous roll to the sea, free of everything this world has to offer. The river ever rolling onwards towards the Gulf and not minding of the rain or the seasons or the wants or demands of the men who ply the waters without any understanding their literal depths.

The Man of the Waters, the eternal river are all calling to her from beneath the waves to a forever home with the Ol' Blues Man's bittersweet song humming in her ears. This new tune is making her almost miss the damn haunting tune he usually reserved for her. She smiles her last crooked wicked smile as tears fill her eyes for the first time in forever, as she sinks knee deep into the river.

Hello my lovely, The Man of the Waters greets her when she's hip deep in his waters.

She smiles beneath the depth and warmness of his voice, the calmness of the river influencing her the deeper she wades into the river and it settles over her.

Beloved, embrace me my sweetly.
Become eternal my love.
Come home to me my beloved goddess.

The waters of the river take her in easily and she disappears without a sound or ripple beneath them. It is a stunning lack of dramatic impact after all she'd wrought over the past seven years. After all she'd writ large in letters of blood, carnage, and violence as opposed to this decidedly anticlimactic ending here.

There should be a sharp crack of thunder or something. A cry out from the world or the city at the loss. Nature is said to abhor a vacuum, so there should at least be a rush of sound to fill the suddenly absent space vacated. But there's nothing to note the passing of the Haunt other than eerie silence.

The distant noise from the Quarter finally drifts over to cover the spot where she'd disappeared as if nothing of note has happened at all here on this spot as time ticks on in its endless march. The eternal river bends towards its rendezvous with the open sea as a haunting harp blows its tunes out over the never still waters which are always moving away from the world of men.

White flowers are cast after her from an unknown hand to mark the spot where she sank into the depths of the big muddy river. Gone missing if not forgotten until the next time the city needs a haunt raised.

Bride of the River, her last title, her last and best name. A name accepted now as her own as she's lost beneath the waters, timeless now and ancient joined with The Man of The Waters, a haunt no more..

ABOUT THE AUTHOR

Jack Kelly is a pseudonym.

THE TERRIBLE FRIGHT
is the third book,

completing the triptych

Begun with **RISE A HAUNT**

And continued in

WAKE THE DEAD

You Saw Her Start   **See Her Continue**

Both books are available at Amazon.com and Kindle